# This Preston Pig Story

## Belongs To:

. . . . . . . . . .

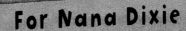

For Nana Dixie

First published in Great Britain in 1995 by
Andersen Press Ltd., 20 Vauxhall Bridge Road, London
SW1V 2SA. This paperback edition first published
in 2008 by Andersen Press Ltd.
Published in Australia by Random House Australia Pty.,
Level 3, 100 Pacific Highway, North Sydney, NSW 2060.
Copyright © Colin McNaughton, 1995.
The rights of Colin McNaughton to be identified as the
author and illustrator of this work have been asserted
by him in accordance with the Copyright, Designs and
Patents Act, 1988. All rights reserved. Colour separated
in Switzerland by Photolitho AG, Zürich.
Printed and bound in Singapore by Tien Wah Press.

10  9  8  7  6  5  4  3  2  1

British Library Cataloguing in Publication Data available.

ISBN 978 1 84270 718 0

This book has been printed on acid-free paper

Through the dark, dark streets of the dark, dark town, Preston (the Masked Avenger) sneaks...

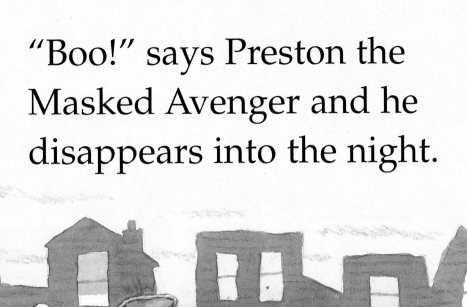

"Boo!" says Preston the Masked Avenger and he disappears into the night.

Slinking through the shadows,
Preston the Masked Avenger
spies Billy the Bully,
his next victim...

"Boo!" says Preston the Masked Avenger and he disappears into the night.

Cat-like, Preston the Masked Avenger slides through the darkness until he reaches the school-house where his teacher is working late...

"Boo!" says Preston the Masked Avenger and he disappears into the night.

Next, the super-hero
comes to Mr Wolf's house.
"Boo!" says Preston the Masked
Avenger very quietly and
he sneaks right past.
"I may be a super-hero," says
Preston, "but I'm not daft!"
And he disappears
into the night.

MR.WOLF

NO
WOOD
CUTTERS

Preston the Masked Avenger
lies in wait for the greatest
villain in the universe – his dad.

"Boo!" says Preston the Masked Avenger and he disappears into the night.

(At least, he would have done if his dad hadn't grabbed him first.)

"Preston!" says Preston's dad. "I've had complaints about you from all over town. You're a naughty little pig."

Preston the Unmasked
Avenger is sent to his room
without any supper.

# Suddenly!

"Boo!" says Preston's dad.
"That'll teach you to go
around scaring people."

But it doesn't.

# Look out for more Preston Pig Stories:

Colin McNaughton

Suddenly!

A Preston Pig Story